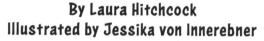

BE BRAVE LIKE AQUAMAN!

By Laura Hitchcock

Illustrated by Jessika von Innerebner

Aquaman created by Paul Norris and Mort Weisinger

The editors would like to thank Robert Seaver, MD,
for his assistance in the preparation of this book.

A Random House PICTUREBACK® Book

Random House 🏠 New York

Copyright © 2019 DC Comics.
DC SUPER FRIENDS and all related characters and elements
© & ™ DC Comics. WB SHIELD: ™ & © Warner Bros. Entertainment Inc.
(s19)

RHUS41314

ISBN 978-1-9848-4831-4 (trade) — ISBN 978-1-9848-4832-1 (ebook)
MANUFACTURED IN CHINA
10 9 8 7 6 5 4 3 2 1

This *BE BRAVE* book belongs to

_____

Most people love to swim.
But some people need a little encouragement—
even super heroes!

Aquaman is a super hero who can swim incredibly fast—and he can talk to fish!

But did you know that Aquaman grew up on land? He had to learn to be brave in water.

You can learn to be brave in water, too!
Just start slowly and take your time.

When Aquaman needs help, he reaches out to his pals, the other Super Friends.

You have amazing friends, too!
Being nervous around water is common—
so talk to your friends or a grown-up.

There are lots of ways to have fun near water, even if you don't jump in.

The Super Friends use different gadgets in and around water when they're on rescue missions.

The Super Friends use tools and teamwork
to stay safe and get the job done!

Before diving in, super heroes put on
the right suit and pack the right gear
for the mission.

Swim goggles let you open your eyes
so you can see underwater. Earplugs keep
water out of your ears!

To help you float, put on a life vest. Have an adult make sure it's buckled correctly and feels snug.

And don't forget sunscreen!

A sunburn can take down
even the mightiest hero!

Now it's time for swim lessons—even heroes need lessons! Your parents can find a class with a good teacher or coach.

Remember, Aquaman never goes
into battle alone . . .

. . . and you should never be in water alone. Always swim with a parent or other adult.

And make sure
a lifeguard is nearby
in case you need help.

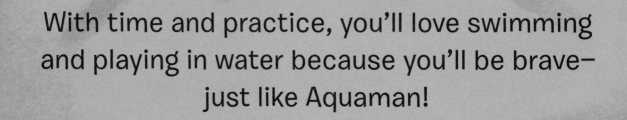

With time and practice, you'll love swimming
and playing in water because you'll be brave—
just like Aquaman!